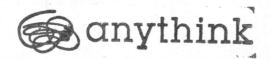

*"Like three silent moons...pulling the three through the night."*

Annette von Droste-Hülshoff

## To Eva-Maria

List of items:

- Les Tres Riches Heures du Duc de Berry, extracts, December, January, Paul and Jean de Limbourg, 1410-1411, Musée Condé in Chantilly, France (pages 2-3 and 30-31)
- The Adoration of the Magi, Gentile da Fabriano, 1423, Uffizi Gallery, Florence, Italy (cover picture and pages 16-17, 20, 22, 23, 25 and 27)
- The Journey of the Magi, Abraham Cresques, 1375 Catalan Atlas, National Library of France, Paris (pages 5, 12 and 4th cover)
- The Adoration of the Magi, Andrea Mantegna, 1495, Paul Getty Museum, Los Angeles, USA (page 7)
- The Adoration of the Magi, detail, Rogier van der Weyden, 1455, Alte Pinakothek, Munich, Germany (page 8)
- Astronomical sky painted on the ceiling of the Chapel of the Sacristy of San Lorenzo Vecchia, Giuliano Pesello, 1442, Florence, Italy (page 9)
- The Adoration of the Magi, detail, fresco, Giotto di Bondone, 1305, Scrovegni Chapel, Padua, Italy (page 10)
- The Procession of the Magi, detail, Benozzo Gozzolli, Chapel of the Medici Palace, Florence, Italy (pages 11, 13, 15)
- Massacre of the Innocents, detail, fresco, Giotto di Bondone, 1305, Scrovegni Chapel, Padua, Italy (page 14)
- The Adoration of the Shepherds, detail, Domenico Ghirlandaio, 1485, Santa Trinita, Florence, Italy (page 19)
- Epiphany Triptych, central panel, detail, Hieronymus Bosch, around 1495, Prado Museum, Madrid, Spain (page 21)
- Shrine of the Three Kings, Nicolas of Verdun, 1181-1230, Cologne Cathedral, Germany (pages 28, 29)

## minedition

English editions published 2016 by Michael Neugebauer Publishing Ltd., Hong Kong

Text copyright © 2013 Géraldine Elschner
Translated by Kathryn Bishop, English text.
© Alinari Archives, Florence, for the cover image and the images of pages 7, 8, 9, 10, 14, 15, 19, 20,27, 28 and 29
© Bridgeman, Paris, for the fourth image coverage and those on pages 2-3, 5, 11, 12, 13, 16-17, 18, 21, 22, 23, 25 and 30-31
Rights arranged with "minedition" Rights and Licensing AG, Zurich, Switzerland.

Michael Neugebauer Publishing Ltd., Unit 23, 7F, Kowloon Bay Industrial Centre, 15 Wang Hoi Road, Kowloon Bay, Hong Kong. Phone +852 2807 1711, e-mail: info@minedition.com
This edition was printed in July 2016 at L.Rex Printing Co Ltd.
3/F., Blue Box Factory Building, 25 Hing Wo Street, Tin Wan, Aberdeen, Hong Kong, China
Typesetting in Silentium Pro designed by Jovica Veljovic
Library of Congress Cataloging-in-Publication Data available upon request.

ISBN 978-988-8341-26-9

10 9 8 7 6 5 4 3 2 1  First Impression

For more information please visit our website: www.minedition.com

# THE THREE KINGS
## The Journey of the Magi

conceived and retold by Géraldine Elschner
translated by Kathryn Bishop

minedition

Who were they?
Where did they come from?

There were three, it is said, and they
came from far away in the East.

One had a beard like the wise ones of old.
The other was a man in the prime of life,
and the third was still young.
Were they the Magi?
Did they wear conical hats or turbans?
Was the youngest white or black?
When did they come?
No one really knows.
There were many stories told about them,
and many pictures were painted.
Their names were Caspar, Melchior
and Balthasar.

In time, these wise men from the East
became known as kings.
They were noble and generous,
and they were very inquisitive.
Every night, like astronomers,
they watched the vast heavens.
Sun, moon and stars,
constellations and comets,
such a beautiful world, full of magic.

But one night ...

As they were marveling at the Milky Way,
as they had so often done before, the Three
Kings noticed a new star in the heavens.
It shone brighter than all the others.
At once they took maps, compasses, and rulers
and started calculating and recording.
Everything about this star suggested the birth
of a new king, whose arrival had been foretold
by Prophecy.
He would be a king of peace and justice!
So they called their servants, had gifts prepared
and then set about on their way.

They would search for this savior.

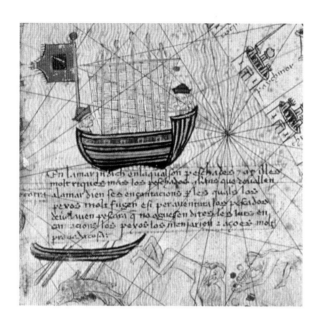

It would be a long journey.
By boat, they crossed the lakes and seas,
delivered by wind and storm.
On horses, they rode through dense forests,
on camels through endless deserts–and always
the bright star in the sky guided them.

A long caravan followed them.

They had just arrived in Judea when the star disappeared.
So the three kings went to Herod, the ruler of the country, visiting him in his magnificent palace, and asked him,

"Where is the new-born king? We have seen his star and have come to worship him."

"A king?" Herod asked, hiding his fear.

"Find out where this child is," Herod asked them.
"And when you have found him, tell me, so I too can welcome him."

In truth, his heart was filled with jealousy.

The three kings continued their journey.
The star that had traveled with them for so long was once
again in the heavens.

The sight filled them with great joy.

Suddenly the bright star seemed to shine over an old wooden shed.

A stable? How could that be? They had expected a royal palace. But there lay the child with his mother, Mary, and Joseph of Nazareth, who watched over him. The Savior had been born on a bed of straw, between the ox and the donkey.

Shepherds who had been keeping watch over their flocks were already there, the first to come to Bethlehem to worship the babe.

Everyone had brought a gift–a warm coat, a little milk and soft wool in a basket. They had even brought a little lamb.

Only the best would do for this child!

When the shepherds moved back, the kings
drew closer and knelt down.
They opened their treasure-boxes and presented
the child with gifts:

the gold of kings,
frankincense, the incense of prayer,
and myrrh of eternity.

Only the most beautiful would do for this child!

These were the first gifts of Christmas.

As Balthasar put down his crown,
Caspar looked at Mary's delicate face.
Who was she, to be the mother of this king?

She was young, almost as young as he was.
She sat pensively, wrapped in her beautiful blue
robe, calmly amidst all the noise, and said nothing.

So much gold, so much honor for her son, whom
she had brought so alone into the world...

Worried, she held him tightly.
He was secure in her arms.

Behind the kings, a crowd had gathered.
There was talking, shoving, scolding and
laughter.

Everyone wanted to see the child.
Everyone wanted a place by the manger.

Even the animals were excited.
What was happening here?
Something special, they sensed it.

At night, in a dream, the kings
were warned.
They should not tell Herod where to
find the new-born baby.
His hatred would endanger the life
of the child.
And so they took another road,
one that led them home,
happy and deeply moved.

One thing was certain...

The old king would never forget the
tiny hand on his head as he held
the little foot of the young king.

*N*ow, amidst the fragrance of incense, the Three Kings from the East rest forever, in a large cathedral, which was built for them a long time ago.

Their relics are preserved in an ornate golden shrine adorned with precious stones in the Cathedral of Cologne. They were brought from Milan in 1164. Since then, visitors from all over the world have come to honor them.

The gifts of the Three Kings are said to be in Greece, on Mount Athos. And so it is that the Wise Men, the Three Kings from the East, have not been forgotten...

Every year, on the sixth of January, a festival is celebrated. It is called Epiphany. In many countries a special cake is baked and others celebrate by parading through the streets. In some places, the night before Epiphany is called Twelfth Night, and celebrations are as they were traditionally– a time for mumming and wassail. Still others go caroling from house to house, dressed as the Three Kings with crowns and a big star, singing and collecting gifts for other children in the world. Gifts that are given in remembrance of the Three Kings.